THE SECRET EXPLORERS
AND THE COMET COLLISION

SJ King

CONTENTS

Chapter One
STARGAZING

Roshni attached her telescope to its stand. Excitement buzzed through her. "I really hope I see it tonight," she said to herself.

She was on the shore of Pangong Lake in India. The water seemed almost as still and quiet as the surface of the moon. Roshni's parents were talking in low voices over by the campfire. The vast Himalayan

Mountains loomed in the distance, their great dark shapes blotting out part of the sky. Overhead, thousands of stars shone like glittering dust.

It was chilly, but Roshni didn't mind. She wasn't scared of the dark, either. She loved it!

In fact, the less light there was, the better. You couldn't see the stars as well in a city, because of the streetlights. But out here, so far from the nearest town, the stars stood out in brilliant pinpoints. *This is the perfect place to stargaze*, thought Roshni.

She finished setting up her telescope and peered through the lens. It wasn't a toy—it was a real scientific instrument, and almost three feet long. Roshni was very proud of it. Down the side, she'd written her favorite saying: *The night hides a world, but reveals a universe.*

She carefully adjusted the telescope and a planet shone brightly against the dark.

"I can see you, Jupiter!" she whispered, and grinned. "Hi there, big guy."

It was June, the time of year when Jupiter's orbit brought it closest to Earth. Roshni had seen Jupiter before, but never this clearly. She could even make out its colored bands.

What Roshni really wanted to see was the enormous storm on Jupiter's surface. This was called the Great Red Spot. Roshni imagined that it would look like the eye of an angry giant! But she couldn't zoom in any farther.

She sighed. Her beloved telescope just wasn't powerful enough.

"I know!" she said. "My new lens!" Her parents had bought it for her to improve her telescope. Could it make Jupiter's image big enough to see the Great Red Spot?

She jumped up from the telescope, ran over to her little tent—and stopped in her tracks.

A compass symbol had appeared on her tent flap. It was glowing.

Roshni knew that symbol well. Pinned to her jacket was a badge in the exact same shape—the sign of the Secret Explorers!

Grinning to herself, Roshni scrambled through the tent flaps and into brilliant white light. Wind whistled through her hair and ruffled her jacket. She felt as if she were

plunging as fast as a meteor through the sky.

A couple of seconds later, the light faded. Roshni looked around. She was surrounded by the familiar black stone walls of the Exploration Station, which gleamed like mirrors. A row of computer screens flickered.

"Roshni—here!" she yelled.

The only other person around was Tamiko, who was arranging some fossils in a display cabinet. "Hi!" Tamiko called and waved to her.

Roshni waved back. "Dinosaur bones?"

"Of course!" Tamiko said with a grin. She was the Dinosaur Explorer.

Roshni couldn't wait to find out why the Secret Explorers had been summoned this time. She jumped onto the huge, squishy sofa to watch the others arrive.

9

Overhead, on the domed ceiling, was an image of the Milky Way. On the floor was a huge map of the world. As the Secret Explorers came running through the glowing doorway, tiny lights flashed up from one country after another, showing where they were arriving from.

"Connor—here!" Connor waved at Roshni and Tamiko. He was the Marine Explorer and knew all about the oceans.

Leah, the Biology Explorer, bounded in after him. She called her name and did her usual snappy salute. Leah knew all about plants and animals. Then came Ollie, dressed in the dark green shorts and T-shirt he wore to explore the rain forests.

"What's the mission?" Ollie asked.

"The Exploration Station hasn't told us yet," Roshni said.

"Kiki—here!" A girl zoomed through the doorway on a powered skateboard. Kiki was the Engineering Explorer, and Roshni knew she had built the skateboard herself.

Cheng, who was the Geology Explorer, came running in next. He was wearing a T-shirt that featured pictures of various colorful rocks. Gustavo, the History Explorer, followed him in, and the doorway winked shut.

All the Secret Explorers stood in a circle around the map on the floor. Any moment now, the Exploration Station would show them their mission.

Any moment now...

"Nothing's happening," Gustavo said. "The Exploration Station isn't broken, is it?"

"No way," Kiki said sternly.

"There's the answer, guys!" said Cheng with a laugh. He pointed up. "We're all looking in the wrong place."

They all gazed up at the Milky Way glowing on the ceiling. Roshni felt a rush of excitement. It was going to be a space mission—and she was the Space Explorer!

An image appeared among the stars in a little square window. It showed a shiny metal object with a large dish on the front. The object tracked slowly through the starry darkness.

"It's a probe!" Roshni said.

"A what?" asked Leah with a frown.

"A sort of spacecraft with no one on board. It's remote-controlled from a base back on Earth," Roshni explained. "Scientists send probes off into space to find things out. There must be a problem with this one!"

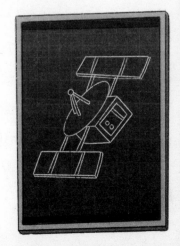

Now that they all knew what the mission was, there was only one more question— who would be picked to go? *I really hope it's me*, thought Roshni. They all stood still, waiting eagerly. Everyone knew that only two lucky Explorers would be chosen.

Roshni's compass badge lit up.

"Yes!" she cheered. "I'm going into space!"

Everyone laughed. "That's no surprise," Tamiko said with a smile. "You are the Space Explorer, after all!"

But it was Ollie whose badge lit up next.

He stared at it. "Uh... Roshni, are there any rain forests in space?"

"Not as far as we know," Roshni said.

"Don't worry," said Connor grinning. "The Exploration Station never gets it wrong. We all know that, right?"

"Right!" they all agreed. Even if they

didn't understand the Exploration Station's choices, it never let them down.

"Okay, guys. Ready to go?" Kiki rubbed her hands together. "I love this part!"

She went to the control panel and pushed a huge red button.

With a shudder of machinery, a platform rose up from below the floor. Sitting in the middle was a battered old go-kart with two plastic seats. It was named the Beagle, after the ship sailed by the great scientist Charles Darwin. The Secret Explorers knew that their Beagle was much more impressive than it looked.

All the Explorers who weren't going on the mission went and sat by their computers. The screens lit up, showing images of the solar system. Roshni knew that if she and Ollie needed any help during their mission, they could always call upon their friends.

BEEP-BOOP, said the Beagle. It seemed to be saying, "Hurry up!"

"Don't worry," Roshni said with a laugh. "We can't wait to get going, either."

She and Ollie climbed into their seats and buckled their safety harnesses. Roshni

took a deep breath and pressed the large, glowing button marked "START."

Instantly, there was a dazzling flash of light. With a deep humming, rattling sound, the Beagle began to transform while they were still sitting in it. The hard plastic seats swelled into padded ones. Banks of controls rose up before their astonished eyes.

The Beagle shot forward into a swirling tunnel of light that had appeared in front of them. It picked up speed, going faster and faster. The light became too bright to look at... and just like that, it faded away again.

Roshni looked around. Window panels, complicated controls, and a joystick had appeared in front of her. Everything was suddenly very quiet. A strange feeling came over her—a sort of floaty lightness.

Outside, stars glinted like diamonds against total blackness.

Her mouth opened with amazement. This was too good to be true.

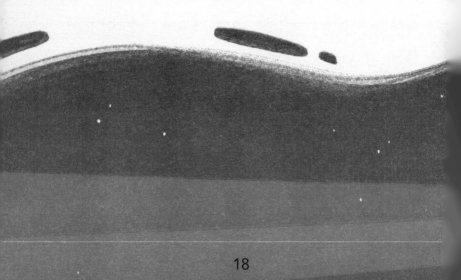

"Is it nighttime already?" Ollie asked. "I can see stars outside."

"That's because we're in space," Roshni said triumphantly. "The Beagle has changed into a spaceship!"

Chapter Two
DANGER INCOMING

With a cheerful beep, a sign lit up that said, "UNFASTEN SEAT BELTS NOW". Roshni and Ollie glanced at each other and quickly undid their buckles.

"Might as well have a look around," Roshni suggested.

"Whoa!" Ollie cried. "What's going on? I'm flying!"

Sure enough, he was gently drifting up into the air. His unfastened seat belt rippled below him like a flag in the wind.

Roshni giggled. "You're not flying. You're floating!"

She pushed down with her hands, and immediately rose upward. Her hair wafted out around her as if she were underwater. It felt pretty strange, but very fun, too.

Ollie chuckled as he waved his arms and legs. "This is awesome!"

"It's because there's hardly any gravity up here," Roshni explained. "Back on Earth, the gravity is strong and pulls everything down.

That's why we don't float away."

"This is much more fun," said Ollie. "I'm going to do a cartwheel." He sent himself spinning across the cabin.

Roshni went one better, and launched into a triple forward somersault.

"Look out!" Ollie warned as Roshni tumbled past him.

CRASH!

She bumped into the side of the cabin and knocked a coil of electrical cable off the wall. But thanks to the special padding all around the inside of the Beagle, it didn't hurt at all. They could zoom around as much as they liked!

They floated around for a while, getting used to the strange weightless feeling. The Beagle helpfully lit up some grab handles that they could hold on to.

"So where are we?" Ollie wondered.

"Space!"

"Sure, but where in space? Mars? Venus? The moon?"

"Let's find out." Roshni reached for a grab handle and pulled herself toward the window.

She gasped. Looming up ahead was a gigantic planet with orange stripes and faint rings. "Jupiter!" she said.

When Roshni had seen the planet through her telescope, it had seemed no bigger than her thumbnail. Now it was so big she couldn't even see all of it.

Ollie whistled. "Now that's a big planet. I bet you could fit Earth inside there at least ten times."

"Try one thousand three hundred times," Roshni said in awe. "It's the biggest planet in the solar system." She grabbed Ollie's arm. "And look! There's the Great Red Spot!"

From this close, Roshni could make out the enormous storm easily. *This definitely makes up for not seeing it earlier*, she thought.

"Wow!" said Ollie. "It's all swirly, like a whirlpool."

There were smaller spots spinning across Jupiter, too. Roshni pointed them out to Ollie.

"They're all storms on Jupiter's surface, like we have on Earth," she explained. "The Great Red Spot's a storm as well. It's been going on for hundreds of years." She pointed to a tiny shining object. "Jupiter's got moons like we have, too."

Ollie's eyebrows shot up. "Moons? You mean, more than one?"

Roshni grinned and showed him more little objects. "That's a moon. And so's that, and that."

"Seriously?" Ollie asked. "How many moons does Jupiter have?"

"Oh, more than seventy," Roshni said casually.

Ollie stared at her. "Seventy?"

"Yep," said Roshni. "And the rings, of course."

"Wait, what?" Ollie peered through the window. "I thought it was just Saturn that had rings."

"Look more closely," said Roshni.

Sure enough, there were ghostly rings around Jupiter. They were faint and easy to miss at first.

"They look a bit like when light shines through dust," Ollie said.

"That's exactly what they're made from," said Roshni. "They're dust from Jupiter's moons."

The view of Jupiter wobbled as the Beagle rocked from side-to-side. The console let out a **BRUP-BOOP** sound. Roshni and Ollie looked at one another. It sounded like the Beagle was saying, "Uh-oh!"

"Something's wrong," Roshni said.

BREEE! replied the Beagle, and made a jangly noise like a mouse running up and down an electronic keyboard.

Using the handles on the walls, Roshni and Ollie clambered down to the navigation display. A blinking red dot was heading in their direction, fast.

Roshni tapped the screen to see what it was, and the display zoomed in. It showed a huge rock, easily three times the size of the Beagle.

"It's an asteroid!" she cried. "No wonder the Beagle is worried. We need to steer clear of that thing or it could smash right through the hull!"

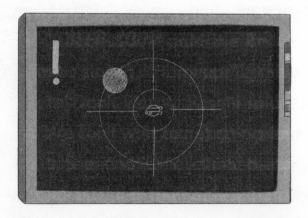

As quickly as they could, they climbed back into their seats and buckled themselves in tight.

Ollie turned to Roshni, looking anxious. "This might be a silly question, but... have you actually flown a spaceship before?"

"Only in my dreams," Roshni admitted.

She looked over the controls. She was sure she could figure out what to do, if she had enough time. But time was running out!

The Beagle blared a warning siren. Red lights flashed on the control console.

In the distance, the asteroid came into view, tumbling end over end. Roshni gulped.

"A little help here, Beagle?" she yelled.

Shiny arrow-shaped lights lit up, pointing to the controls they needed to use. Roshni took hold of the joystick, while Ollie grabbed the thruster levers that would power the spaceship forward. More lights sparked into life. There were switches to flick, buttons to press, and dials to turn.

All the time, the asteroid was coming closer and closer...

"We need to turn the nose to the left, then hit the thrusters," Roshni said.

"Got it," Ollie replied.

The Beagle beeped even louder than before. Now it was really worried. It sounded like an ambulance and a fire engine racing each other.

"Hang on, Beagle! We're doing our best!"

Roshni said through clenched teeth.

Using the joystick, she carefully nudged the spaceship's nose to the left. That should do it.

But to her horror, the ship kept on turning. If she didn't do something, it would just spin around on the spot!

She pushed the joystick the other way, just enough to stop the Beagle from spinning.

"Oh, no!" Ollie wailed. Roshni looked up.

The asteroid loomed up ahead of them, blotting out Jupiter. It was coming at them as fast as a speeding train.

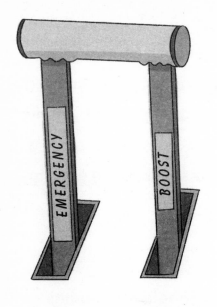

"Full thrust, now!" she yelled. Ollie gritted his teeth and quickly hauled the big thruster controls down. Roshni yanked a lever labeled "EMERGENCY BOOST."

The Beagle shuddered as its powerful rocket engines roared into life. Roshni and Ollie were flung backward in their seats.

The asteroid went spinning past, so close it almost knocked off their tail fin.

They picked up speed. Soon the asteroid was far behind them—just a speck vanishing in the distance.

The Beagle made a happy *BEEP*. Roshni and Ollie cheered and slapped their hands together in a high five.

"That was way too close," Roshni said. "I don't mind studying space dust, but I don't want to *become* space dust!"

Chapter Three
TROUBLE IN SPACE

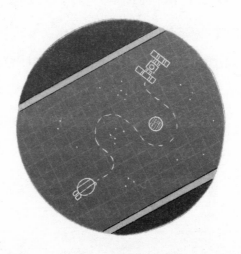

"Time to get on with the mission," said Roshni. A space probe needed the Secret Explorers' help. They didn't know what kind of help, but they knew it was urgent.

"Where's the probe?" Ollie asked.

Roshni peered out into space. "I can't see it. Hey, Beagle, can you scan for the probe?"

The Beagle was quiet for a few seconds.

Lights went on and off. Then it beeped a triumphant *TA-DAAAH!* An image of the probe appeared on the navigation display, as well as directions to reach it.

Roshni carefully pointed the Beagle's nose the right way and Ollie fired the rockets. Steadily, the spacecraft changed course.

"Flying a spaceship isn't as easy as it looks in the movies, is it?" Ollie said.

"That's because in space, if you set off in one direction, you continue moving that way and don't stop," Roshni explained. "You can't hit the brakes like you would in a car."

"So how do you slow down?"

"You have to turn on thrusters that fire in the opposite direction, so the movement cancels out," said Roshni.

"Got it," said Ollie. He turned to the navigation display. "Looks like we're heading the right way," he said. Next to the image of the probe, a distance counter was ticking down.

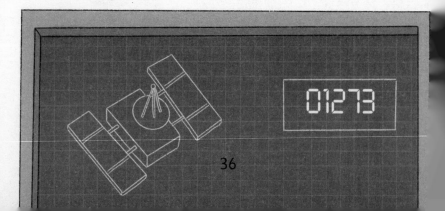

Something huge, gray, and round appeared in the distance. *Another asteroid?* wondered Roshni. *No—it's far too big!*

She quickly nudged the controls to steer them safely past it. As it rushed closer, she could make out craters on the surface.

"Hey, that looks like the moon!" Ollie said.

"It's a moon, all right," said Roshni. She'd figured out what they were looking at. "That's Ganymede, the biggest of Jupiter's moons."

"Is it bigger than our moon?"

Roshni laughed. "It's bigger than Mercury!"

"But Mercury's a planet!" Ollie said. "Wow! Seems like everything about Jupiter is king-size."

"That makes sense," Roshni said. "Jupiter gets its name from the king of the Roman gods, after all."

The Beagle made urgent little *BIP-BIP-BIP* noises. Roshni noticed that the distance counter was nearly at zero.

"We've almost reached the probe!" she said. "We need to slow down now. The Beagle should have retro-rockets somewhere—they fire in the direction a spaceship is flying, which slows it down."

"Got them!" Ollie pulled a lever. "Retro-rockets... fired!" he said. Steadily, the Beagle slowed to a complete stop.

The probe floated in space in front of them, gleaming in the light from the cockpit.

It looked very tiny against the gigantic planet in the background.

Roshni felt a sense of wonder at how far it had come. *It's probably been ten years since it blasted off from Earth*, she thought. *That's how long it takes to fly to Jupiter*. And now something had gone wrong. But what could it be?

She took a good long look at the probe.
If only she'd brought some of her books on
space exploration with her. The illustrations
would have come in handy right now...

"There are the thrusters," she said, "and
there's the power generator... and the
camera. They all look fine. Oh, no! Ollie,
look. The antenna is gone!"

"The what?" Ollie asked.

"The antenna. Space probes collect information, remember?" Roshni said. "But it's no good if the information just stays here on the probe. It has to be sent back to Earth."

"So the scientists can study it," said Ollie. "Hey, what do you think that's for?"

A clock had appeared on the control console. Bright red numbers flickered as it counted down the minutes and seconds.

"It looks like we've got just under two hours before something happens," Roshni said. She frowned. "But what?"

"It can't be a warning about the asteroid," Ollie said, "because we've already dodged it. Beagle, what's this countdown clock for?"

But all the Beagle did was beep noisily.

"The Beagle sounds pretty impatient," Roshni said. "Ollie, do you think the countdown has something to do with the probe?"

Ollie shrugged. "I don't know. And I don't think we're going to figure this one out on our own."

"You mean..."

Ollie nodded.

"Let's call the Exploration Station!" they said together.

Roshni operated the communications control. "Beagle calling the Secret Explorers! Do you copy? This is Roshni. We need help!"

There was silence for a second. Roshni bit her knuckles. Could the Beagle reach their friends back on Earth in time to fix the probe?

Then a crackly voice came through the speakers. "Leah here! Go ahead, Roshni. What's the problem?"

On the console, a screen flickered. Then an image of the Exploration Station appeared. Good work, Beagle! All the Secret Explorers were gathered around Leah's computer. They listened carefully as Roshni explained what was happening.

"Okay, everyone, go!" Connor said. "Research everywhere you can. Websites, records, the works. Roshni and Ollie are counting on us!"

Roshni and Ollie watched their friends eagerly. The Secret Explorers hurried to the other computer screens. Keyboards rattled as they typed, hunting for all the information they could find.

After only a few minutes, Roshni saw Cheng switch on his microphone. "Roshni, can you hear me?"

"Go ahead, Cheng," she replied.

"The probe's name is Odin," said Cheng. "Its mission is to watch a comet collide with Jupiter. The countdown clock is to tell you how long you have left before the comet hits. If you don't get it fixed in time..."

"... the probe's data will be lost," said Roshni. "And the scientists' work sending the probe into space will all be for nothing!"

Cheng nodded. "Good luck," he said.

"We know you can do it," added Kiki.

"Thanks for your help, guys," said Ollie. "Beagle out." He switched the radio off.

"We need to hurry," cried Roshni. "There are less than two hours left on the clock!" Frantically, she pressed switches and buttons. "There's no antenna, and the comet's coming, and we need to pix the frobe... I mean fix the probe..."

"Slow down," Ollie said. "Take deep breaths and imagine you're in a beautiful rain forest. It's what I do."

Roshni closed her eyes. She pictured tall, leafy trees—and felt much calmer. She opened her eyes again. "Thanks, Ollie!" She turned to the navigation screen. "Beagle," she said, "can you scan for the missing antenna like you scanned for the probe before?"

The Beagle beeped a cheery tune while its scanning dish whirred back and forth. **PING!** The antenna appeared on the screen.

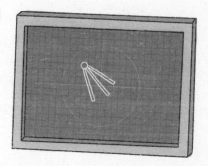

Roshni patted the console. "Nice job, Beagle." She peered through the window at a distant moon. It was white with red-brown streaks on its surface. "Looks like the antenna's in orbit around Europa."

"It's in Europe?" Ollie said. "You mean, back on Earth?"

"Not Europe! Europa, with an 'a' on the end." Roshni showed him. "It's nearly as big as Ganymede."

With the Beagle's help, Roshni and Ollie set a course for Europa.

As the little spacecraft zoomed toward it, Roshni glanced at the countdown clock. She shivered all over. Only an hour and a half left!

We've still got to grab that antenna and attach it to the Odin probe, thought Roshni. *Can we really do it in such a short time?*

Chapter Four
ONE GIANT LEAP...

Europa grew larger and larger as the Beagle drew closer. It looked like a frosty round ball against the endless blackness of space.

Roshni fired the retro-rockets to slow them down, and the Beagle began to orbit around the huge moon.

Ollie looked down at Europa's craggy surface. "I wouldn't go there for my vacation.

It looks like it's covered in ice."

"It is," Roshni said. "But it's only frozen on the surface. There are saltwater oceans under the ice."

Ollie raised his eyebrows. "Like we have on Earth?" he asked.

Roshni nodded. "Yes! And better still, scientists think there might even be some simple life-forms swimming around down there."

Ollie's mouth gaped open. "You mean... aliens?" he said.

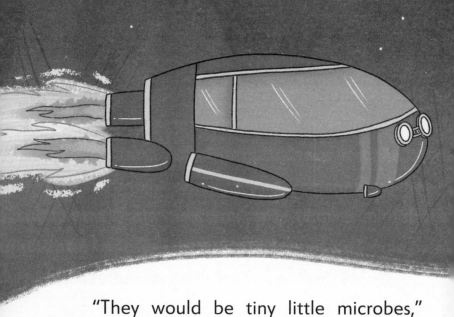

"They would be tiny little microbes," Roshni explained. "You wouldn't be able to see them without a microscope. But, yes— we might be flying over alien life!" She got goose bumps just thinking about it.

"Cool!" Ollie spotted something and peered closer. "What's that thing? Did the aliens build it?"

Roshni saw it, too. It looked like a metal umbrella. She sat bolt upright. "That's the antenna from the Odin probe! Come on, we need to get it back!"

Working fast, the two of them flew the Beagle as close to the antenna as they could. They were getting more used to the controls now.

The antenna tumbled through space, high above the surface of Europa. Roshni wished she could just open a window and grab it, but that wasn't possible in a spaceship. All the air would rush out. This was going to be tricky.

"How are we going to get it?" Ollie wondered.

The Beagle made urgent beeps and wobbled around, jostling Roshni and Ollie in their seats.

"It's trying to tell us something!" Roshni said. "What is it, Beagle? Should we use a robot arm?"

FNAAARP! said the Beagle irritably.

"Can we pull it in with a tractor beam, or something?" Ollie guessed.

The Beagle flashed red lights in a big "X" on the dashboard and buzzed like computer-game sound effects.

No matter what Roshni and Ollie guessed, the Beagle just got more frustrated. It didn't want them to get the antenna with a harpoon gun, a big magnet, or a wad of chewing gum on the end of a string.

Roshni was rapidly running out of ideas— and the antenna was slowly dropping down toward Europa. If they didn't grab it in time, it would smash to pieces. She looked around the Beagle's cockpit to see if they'd missed anything.

Over to the right, she found a door she hadn't noticed before. She pressed a button and it slid open.

Inside was a compartment that was as tall as she was, containing two white space suits with round helmets.

"Wow!" she said.

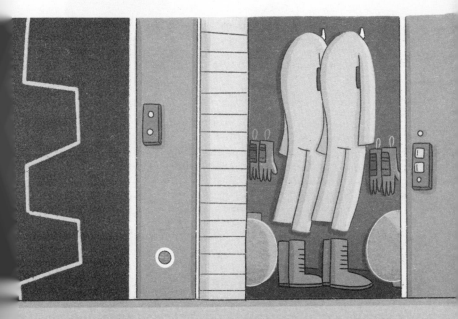

The Beagle made a very relieved beep. It sounded a lot like, "About time..."

Roshni and Ollie looked at one another. Roshni knew her friend was thinking the same thing—one of them had to stay inside the Beagle, but the other would have to put on a space suit and go outside, into space. It was dangerous, but it was also the chance of a lifetime.

"I'll go," they both said.

Ollie looked thoughtful for a moment. Then he said, "Actually, you should go, Roshni. You're the Space Explorer!"

Roshni grinned. "Thanks!"

She climbed out of her seat and slid her legs into the crumpled, shiny space suit. The Beagle lit up a panel that said "SAFETY INSTRUCTIONS." Ollie read them and made sure Roshni's suit was correctly prepared.

Roshni put her helmet on. Ollie checked that it was completely sealed. Even the tiniest gap or hole could result in Roshni's air supply being sucked out. She was breathless already, from sheer excitement. She could hardly believe this was real. She was about to do a space walk!

"This is your safety tether, okay?" said Ollie. He held up a long cable. One end was securely fastened to the middle of Roshni's space suit, and the other ended in a clip. "Make sure the cable is always locked in place," Ollie said. "Then I can pull you back into the Beagle if anything goes wrong."

"Got it!" said Roshni.

The Beagle's airlock was behind the seats. Roshni knew an airlock was a chamber with an inner and an outer set of doors. You only ever opened one set at a time. This was to stop the air from leaving the spaceship.

She pulled the lever and the inner door opened with a hiss. She stepped into the cramped little chamber and closed the inner door behind her. Before she did anything else, she clipped her safety tether to the anchor point inside the airlock. Even if she got separated from the ship, the tether meant she'd always find her way back to the Beagle.

"Here we go," she whispered to herself. She remembered what Neil Armstrong had said when he became the first human being to walk on the moon: *One small step for a man, one giant leap for mankind...* A thrill passed through Roshni.

She pulled the second lever. Air rushed out of the airlock and the outer doors rumbled open.

There, in front of her, was the endless reach of starry space. She floated for a moment, just staring at it all in wonder.

Time to get on with the mission. The clock was ticking.

"One small step for a girl," Roshni murmured. "One giant leap for the Secret Explorers..."

She clambered unsteadily out of the airlock, using the outside of the Beagle like a jungle gym. It turned out to be trickier than she'd expected. The trouble with such little gravity was there was no such thing as "up"!

Roshni wasn't sure if it felt more like climbing up out of a hole, or sideways out of a door.

The antenna hung suspended in space only a few feet above the ship's nose. Roshni carefully worked her way toward it.

She had never seen such a spectacular view in all her life. Below her was the frozen, streaked surface of Europa, and away in the far distance was a shining dot. Roshni knew this was Saturn, the second biggest planet in the solar system.

The cockpit was below her now. She could see Ollie's anxious face looking out at her.

After carefully climbing across the outside of the Beagle, she finally got as close to the antenna as she could. She hung on to the Beagle with one hand and stretched up to grab the antenna with the other. But it was just out of reach.

She tried again, hoping to grab hold of the rim of its dish, but her gloved fingers closed on nothingness.

It was no good. Unless she let go of the Beagle, she'd never reach it.

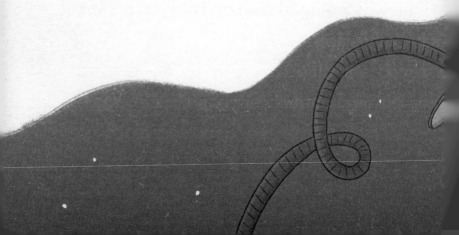

Roshni took a deep breath. She put her hands behind herself and pushed, as if she were launching off the edge of a swimming pool. She floated up in the direction of the antenna. The safety cable spooled out behind her.

Almost there. Just a little farther...

She stretched out toward the antenna with both hands—and grabbed it!

Chapter Five
SPACE SLINGSHOT

Roshni held the antenna tightly to her body. It was the same length as her arm. Up close, it looked even more like an umbrella.

Through the window of the Beagle, Roshni could see Ollie grinning and giving her a thumbs-up. She gave him one back.

"Just one problem now," she said to herself. "I've only got one hand free! So how am

I going to climb back inside the Beagle?"

A moment later, her question was answered. Her safety tether began to pull her back in. Ollie must have pressed the "RECALL" switch! She relaxed and let herself be reeled into the airlock, just like a fish on a line being pulled to shore.

In no time, she passed through the outer airlock doors. She shut them behind her and waited for the airlock to fill up with air again before unfastening her safety tether from the wall.

The inner doors slid open. There was Ollie, waiting with open arms. He gave her a hug. Roshni let go of the antenna so she could squeeze him back with sheer delight.

"You did a space walk!" he said. "That is so unbelievably cool!"

"I know," Roshni said happily. "I'll never forget it as long as I live."

In the background, the Beagle made happy burbling noises and blew a little trumpet fanfare.

"We'd better hurry back to the probe and repair it," Roshni said. "We've only got another thirty minutes before the comet's due to strike Jupiter."

She sat down at the controls and Ollie joined her. They set their course, fired the thrusters, and hoped they'd reach the Odin probe in time.

Through the window, they saw a cluster of shining shapes in the far distance. They were hurtling down toward the planet, leaving foggy trails behind them.

"There's the comet!" Roshni said.

"But it's all broken into bits," Ollie said, looking anxious. "Are we too late?"

"No," Roshni said excitedly. "Comets break up when they get close to a planet, because its gravity pulls them apart. This one must have broken up when it got close to Jupiter."

She checked the distance indicator. They were still nowhere near the probe. Only twenty minutes left to go!

"Can you go any faster, Beagle?" Roshni asked.

The Beagle made a sad beep.

Ollie patted the console. "It's okay. We know you're trying your best."

Roshni racked her brains. They needed to go faster. But how? She remembered watching an online video with her dad about space travel. She thought back to the part about something called "gravity assists"...

"That's it!" she yelled. "We can do a slingshot!"

"Sounds cool," said Ollie. "But what is it, exactly?"

"It's when we get caught in a planet or a moon's orbit on purpose, so we can speed up," Roshni said. "Scientists do it all the time with space probes, to save on fuel."

"I don't understand." Ollie frowned. "If we get caught in a planet's gravity, won't that slow us down?"

Roshni thought hard about how to explain it. "Okay. Say we're at a playground. I'm zipping around on my skates and you're going around in circles on a great big merry-go-round. Are you with me so far?"

"I guess," Ollie said.

"If I skate up behind you and you grab my hand for a second, and then let go, what happens?"

"I whiz you around for a little bit, then you zoom off really fast in a new direction!" Ollie burst out. "I get it. I'm the planet going

around the sun, and me grabbing your hand
is like gravity pulling you in."

"Exactly! Just like a planet giving a probe
a speed boost."

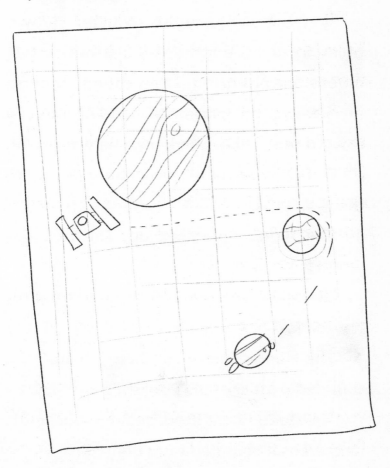

Ollie bent over the navigation screen. "So, all we have to do is find something that's already orbiting Jupiter and hitch a ride. Hey, how about this? It's got to be big enough."

Roshni looked over his shoulder. He was pointing at Io, another of Jupiter's largest moons. She hesitated. If they changed course now, they'd no longer be heading directly toward the probe. She knew she was taking a risk. But if she didn't, they might never get there on time.

She made her mind up. The risk was worth it.

"Beagle," she said, "can you steer us toward Io?"

The Beagle made a cheery beep that sounded a lot like "okeydokey!"

The steering jets fired, and the spacecraft lurched as it changed direction.

Roshni and Ollie watched Io appear in the distance. It grew larger with every passing second. Roshni gripped the joystick tightly. They needed to get caught in Io's gravity for long enough to speed up, then escape it again.

"We've got to time this just right," she said. "Too early, and we'll just shoot past. Too late, and the probe will get to watch us crashing..."

The Beagle bibbled nervously. Ollie stood by with his hand on the thruster control. The whole spacecraft vibrated as the engines thundered.

Roshni's mouth was dry. She steered the Beagle so it would come as close to Io as she dared. "Almost... almost... and here we go! Entering orbit now."

Io's gravity caught the little spacecraft in its grasp. Roshni and Ollie saw Io's surface zoom past them, blindingly fast.

On the dashboard, their velocity counter began to climb up and up, past the maximum limit and even higher.

"Punch it, Ollie!" she shouted.

Ollie hit the thrusters.

The Beagle broke free of Io's gravity and shot away.

They went screaming through space at mind-boggling speed. The velocity counter just read "ERROR." The Beagle squealed with delight.

Roshni held the joystick in a tight grip. Even though they were going so fast, time had almost run out. If they didn't reach the probe soon, all the work that had gone into it would be lost. And there would be no second chances...

Chapter Six
RACE AGAINST TIME

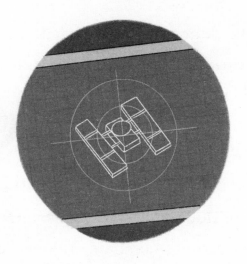

The Odin probe appeared on the scanner. Roshni watched anxiously as they hurtled toward it. They might make it in time... but it would be close!

The Beagle beeped a little tune as it rocketed along. "That slingshot move sped us up, but I think we might have overdone it," said Ollie. His eyes were wide. "We're going too fast!"

"Beagle, we need to slow down," Roshni warned.

The Beagle whined back at her. It clearly didn't want to slow down. It was too excited!

"I know you're having fun, but remember the mission!" she said.

With a sad-sounding beep, the Beagle turned on the retro-rockets. The velocity counter stopped flashing wildly and started to show actual numbers again. Gradually, their speed dropped until they were hovering at a standstill, right beside the gleaming Odin probe.

Ollie glanced at the mission timer. "Fifteen minutes left. Can you fix the probe in that time?"

"If I'm fast," Roshni replied. She was already pulling her helmet back on. "Wish me luck!"

Ollie grabbed her a tool kit from a compartment overhead. Roshni tucked it under her left arm, holding the antenna in her hand. She kept her right hand free to hold on to the Beagle.

She stood in the airlock and closed the inner doors. She was just reaching for the outer door switch when she remembered her safety tether!

That was a close one, she thought, as she clipped it in place.

"You okay in there?" came Ollie's voice through her helmet speaker.

"All ready," she said. "I didn't know we could talk to each other."

"Yeah, I think the intercom uses the safety tether as a communications cable," Ollie explained.

Knowing that she'd be able to stay in contact with Ollie made Roshni feel more confident.

She opened the outer doors. The probe was right there, hanging in space only a few yards away. Maybe this would be easier than she'd dared to hope.

Keeping a careful hold on the antenna and the tool kit, she pushed herself away from the Beagle.

The probe came within reach. Roshni grabbed one of the stronger-looking struts. Once she was sure she was secure, she moved the antenna into place.

She could see exactly what had happened. The antenna was held on by a sort of grip, and it was buckled and twisted where a meteor must have struck it. She'd have to replace it. Luckily, the tool kit had a spare.

"You always make sure we have what we need, don't you, Beagle?" she said fondly.

Ollie was watching her through the window, nervous as a cat in a lightning storm. "Ten minutes," he said.

Roshni focused her mind like never before. She took a wrench from the tool kit and undid the bolts holding the grip that had connected the antenna to the probe.

It was cracked—no wonder the antenna had floated off! Once she'd unscrewed it, the broken grip started to spin away. Roshni caught it and placed it in the tool kit. *Don't want to leave any litter behind*, she thought.

Next, she attached a new grip and bolted it on.

"Eight minutes," said Ollie. "You can do it!"

This next part was all-important. She slotted the antenna into the new grip, making sure the angle was exactly right. If it wasn't pointing the right way, the signals wouldn't reach Earth, and the data would be lost.

She quickly tightened the grip until it was secure.

"All done," she gasped.

She turned to the window, expecting to see Ollie's smiling face. But he wasn't smiling. His face was a mask of terror. His hands were white where they were pressed against the glass.

He yelled, "Roshni, get back to the ship! Now!"

She stared at him. This didn't make any sense.

Then she realized the Beagle was making a **SKREEE** sound of panic, too. *What could have scared them like this?*

She looked around—and in that instant, she had her answer.

As it plunged toward Jupiter, the shattered comet was shedding debris. A storm of tumbling, icy chunks were flying at her! They glittered, sharp as flint, in the light from the Beagle.

"I'm bringing you in," Ollie said firmly. He punched the "RECALL" button.

Roshni felt the reassuring tug of her safety tether pulling her back to the Beagle. She glanced fearfully at the oncoming shower of shards and told herself not to panic.

The first of the shards pinged off her helmet. More of them rattled and zinged around her.

Roshni tried to stay calm and breathe evenly. Soon she'd be back in the safety of the airlock...

"Are you okay?" Ollie said. "Roshni, talk to m—"

His voice cut out.

Roshni drifted toward the airlock door... and right past it.

"Ollie, pull me in!" she yelled. "What's going on? Can you hear me? Ollie!"

Why wasn't he answering?

She looked down. Pure horror ran through her. The safety tether had snapped clean off. One of the razor-sharp comet fragments had sliced right through it.

Now she was slowly drifting farther and farther away from the Beagle. That was how things worked in space, she knew. Once you started moving in one direction, you kept going that way forever and ever...

Roshni gulped. *How am I going to get back to the Beagle now?*

Chapter Seven
LOST IN THE STARS

Roshni was spinning head over heels, as if she were on a crazy fairground ride that she couldn't escape. The stars wheeled around her.

"Don't panic," she said aloud to herself. "Whatever you do, don't panic."

But it was very hard not to, with her stomach doing somersaults and the Beagle drifting steadily away.

Every time she flipped over, she saw the same things pass by. She glimpsed the Beagle, the Odin probe, Jupiter, and the comet fragments about to crash into it. It was making her feel dizzy. If only there were some way she could stop spinning, or something she could grab hold of!

What was it Ollie had said? Imagine you're in a beautiful rain forest. Take deep breaths... Well, it had worked before, hadn't it?

She took a deep breath—and suddenly she realized she was in even more danger than she'd known.

The only air she had to breathe was the air in her suit tanks. She didn't even know how much of it was left after her first space walk. An hour? Or only a few minutes?

"I'm not going to panic," she whispered. "I'm a Secret Explorer. I'll find a way out of this, somehow..."

It didn't seem like things could possibly get any worse. But they did.

She saw the airlock doors on the Beagle close.

Roshni felt cold all over. *Now I'll never get back inside...*

But just as she was on the verge of giving up hope, they opened again. There was Ollie standing in the airlock, wearing the second space suit!

With one hand, he was waving to Roshni. In his other hand, he was holding something like a long rope. *Where did he find that?* Roshni wondered. She hadn't seen a rope on board the Beagle.

Ollie spun the rope's end around and let go of it. It came uncoiling toward Roshni, wobbling and wavering through space. She lost sight of it as she spun all the way over yet again.

As she came back around, she saw the rope was getting closer.

On her next flip, it was closer still.

After one more spin, it would be close enough to catch!

She reached out, her hand open as she turned another full circle. There was the rope, drifting right by her head.

She grabbed the rope, wrapped it around her waist and tied it securely.

"Phew!" she sighed.

Ollie backed into the airlock, where red warning lights were furiously blinking. Roshni watched as he took hold of the rope with both hands and began to pull.

Slowly but surely, Ollie hauled Roshni back toward the airlock.

The moment she was all the way inside, Ollie punched the door control and the outer doors slid shut. The airlock's red warning lights turned green.

Roshni gave him a huge, slightly awkward hug. It wasn't easy to hug someone when you were wearing a big, bulky space suit! Ollie hugged her back as best he could.

The inner doors opened to let them back into the cockpit. The Beagle filled the screens with smiley-face emojis and made happy, excited beeps that sounded like puppies playing.

Roshni pulled her helmet off and shook her hair free. She took a big gasp of air.

"Thanks, Ollie," she said. "I owe you one!"

"Any time," Ollie beamed, taking off his helmet.

Roshni looked down at her waist, where Ollie's rope was still tied. Now she could get a good look at it, she could see it was made of electrical wires wound together. So he hadn't found a spare rope—he'd made one!

"Where did you get the idea to do this?" she asked him.

"In the rain forest. Where else?" He laughed. "We weave vines together to make ropes when we're out exploring. One wire by itself wouldn't have been strong enough to pull you in, but lots of them woven together worked just fine."

Roshni grinned. "See? The Exploration Station always picks the right Explorers for every mission!"

Ollie grinned back.

Together, they looked out of the window at the Odin probe, which had turned to record the comet crash into Jupiter. The comet fragments were zooming toward the gigantic planet.

"We're just in time to see the collision!" said Ollie.

Chapter Eight
JUPITER'S FIREWORKS

Roshni and Ollie had front-row seats for the most spectacular cosmic fireworks display they could ever hope to see. They looked out through the spacecraft's windshield, breathless with excitement. The last few seconds were ticking away on the countdown clock.

"Three, two, one... zero!" Roshni yelled.

The first of the comet fragments plunged into Jupiter's atmosphere. A tremendous fireball erupted at the point of impact. Roshni shielded her eyes. This was amazing!

Enormous shock waves went rippling out across Jupiter's surface, like rings spreading out on a lake.

"How come we can't hear it?" Ollie asked. "An explosion that size ought to be deafening us!"

"Because sound waves need air to travel, and there isn't any air in space," Roshni explained.

The next fragment went tumbling down into the seething storm. Another gigantic explosion went up.

"Look at that," Ollie said. "I bet the ground's shaking down there!"

"Jupiter's not solid—it's made of gas," Roshni said. "It might be solid right at the core, but scientists aren't sure about that. There's a lot scientists don't know about space, which is why they need probes like Odin to do investigations."

Another fireball expanded across Jupiter's surface. Ollie whistled. "Just imagine if a comet hit Earth!"

"A comet did hit Earth, millions of years ago," Roshni explained. "Well, scientists think it was either a comet or a meteorite. That's why the dinosaurs were all wiped out. The impact shook up our entire planet."

"Whoa, really?"

"The crater's still there, in Mexico," Roshni said. "Ask Tamiko about it!"

Outside, the Odin probe was busily collecting data. Its camera was recording image after image, capturing the moment the comet smashed into Jupiter.

That gave Roshni an idea. "Hey, Beagle, can you tune in to the probe's broadcast channel? We might be able to listen in."

BEEEEEEP-BOOP! chirped the Beagle. It sounded like, "Sure thing!"

The computer screens in front of them filled up with information. Roshni grinned. They were getting to watch a science broadcast as it happened and learn cool stats just like the scientists back on Earth!

"Look how fast that comet was going when it hit!" Ollie said. "134,000 miles per hour!"

Roshni's mind boggled. An Olympic athlete running a hundred-meter dash would get up to about 28 miles per hour. The speedometer in her parents' car only went up to about 110 miles per hour. The speed of sound itself was a stunning 767 miles per hour. But the comet was going more than one hundred and seventy times faster than sound!

"No wonder the fragments exploded like that!" she said. "Hey, how hot were those fireballs, anyway?"

Ollie tapped the screen and looked confused. "I'm not sure the probe's working right. These figures are incredible."

"Incredible how?"

"Apparently the temperature down there reached 42,700°F!"

"Forty-two thousand degrees?" Roshni struggled to imagine how hot that was. She knew water boiled at 212°F, but that seemed puny by comparison. So, she said "Beagle, can you show us some temperatures to compare that with?"

The Beagle flashed up some figures for them to read. Iron boiled at 5,184°F—so the comet's impact was about nine times hotter than boiling iron.

"Wow!" Roshni said.

"What about the Earth's core?" Ollie suggested. "That's liquid rock, so it's got to be seriously hot."

They were amazed to see that the center of the Earth measured 10,800°F. The comet explosion was more than four times hotter than the core of their own planet!

"I'm glad we're up here in the Beagle, safely out of the way," Ollie said. "If we were any closer we might be burned to ashes!"

They watched in wonder as the last of the fragments burned up in Jupiter's atmosphere. Roshni saw the information flicker across the screen and smiled. The scientists back on Earth would learn a lot from the probe's data. Maybe what they learned would help humans travel to other planets in the future. Maybe she'd be on one of those spaceships as a grown-up astronaut...

The Beagle beeped. The big button that had read "START" now read "HOME."

"Mission complete," said Roshni. "Time to go back!"

They buckled their safety harnesses and Roshni pressed the button.

Just as it had before, the Beagle shot forward into a tunnel of white light. It was so bright, Roshni could hardly look at it. She thought she could see stars whizzing past, leaving rainbow-colored trails.

Only moments later, the light faded and they slowed to a stop.

The controls and instrument panels were gone. The Beagle was just a go-kart again, with old plastic seats and wacky handlebars. It looked more like something you would find in a backyard shed than a spacecraft that had just been in orbit around Jupiter.

Roshni unfastened her harness and stretched. She looked around the familiar Exploration Station. It was good to be back safe and sound. *But I miss being in space already!* she thought.

All the other Secret Explorers came crowding around. They gave Roshni and Ollie hugs and high fives. Everyone had dozens of questions about the mission.

"Were you scared?" asked Gustavo.

"What was the comet like?" Cheng wanted to know.

"Did you see any aliens?" asked Leah.

Roshni thought of the tiny microbes that might be under the frozen seas of Europa. "Maybe," she said.

"So did you bring anything back for the display cabinets?" Tamiko asked.

Roshni groaned. "Oh, no! I didn't think of that!"

But Ollie leaned over and pulled something from between the Beagle's handlebars. "Hey, Roshni?" he said. "Is this what I think it is?"

He held up a lump of gray ice. It was beginning to melt under the bright lights of the Exploration Station. Inside the ice was a dark shape.

Roshni gasped. "It's a shard of the comet! It must have gotten jammed in the Beagle. I guess we did bring something back after all!"

The ice melted away, revealing a chunk of what looked like dark, bumpy rock. "Wow!" everyone said as they looked at it closely.

"Comets are mostly made of ice," Roshni explained. "But there are minerals and other things inside them, too."

She opened the display cabinet and placed the comet shard inside. It sat between one of Tamiko's fossils and an insect embedded in amber that Ollie had found in the rain forest.

It was time for Roshni to go back to her camping trip. Her parents probably thought she was taking a nap in her tent. *What would they say if they knew I'd been on a space walk?* she thought.

"Goodbye, everyone!" Roshni called. "See you next time!" She waved to her Secret Explorer friends and stepped through the glowing door. She came out the other side and found herself outside her tent. She was back in the Himalayas, by the shores of the lake, encircled by the mountains. Beside the campfire, her parents were still talking—no time had passed while Roshni had been away on her mission.

"Almost forgot what I came to the tent for," she said to herself, and laughed. She ducked inside, then rummaged through her things and found the extra-powerful lens for her telescope.

Her telescope was right where she'd left it—sitting on its tripod and pointing at the sky. She screwed the new lens in and took a fresh look at Jupiter. Much better! The planet stood out bright and clear. The telescope had made it large enough for her to see the Great Red Spot now.

Roshni could hardly believe she'd seen Jupiter up close, and even looked down into its enormous, raging, swirling storm. She wondered what amazing sights her next Secret Explorers adventure would bring.

It was bound to be a big surprise. It always was.

And she couldn't wait for it to begin!

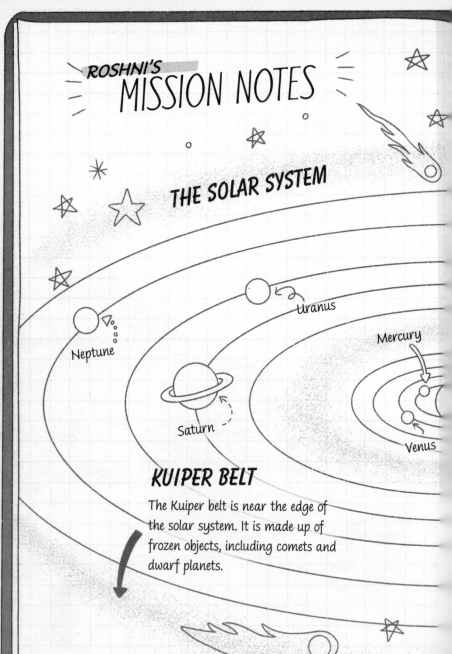

THE SOLAR SYSTEM

Uranus

Mercury

Neptune

Saturn

Venus

KUIPER BELT

The Kuiper belt is near the edge of the solar system. It is made up of frozen objects, including comets and dwarf planets.

The solar system began 4.6 billion years ago. A cloud of gas and dust was pulled together by gravity, eventually becoming a star—our sun. The bits of material left over clumped together into bigger and bigger pieces, forming planets, asteroids, comets, and moons. They all orbit, or travel around, the sun.

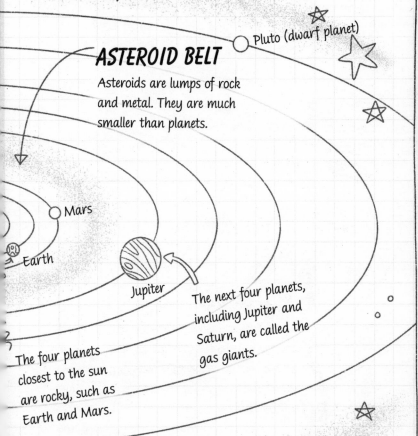

Pluto (dwarf planet)

ASTEROID BELT

Asteroids are lumps of rock and metal. They are much smaller than planets.

Mars

Earth

Jupiter

The next four planets, including Jupiter and Saturn, are called the gas giants.

The four planets closest to the sun are rocky, such as Earth and Mars.

Use this handy phrase to remember the order of the planets from the sun:
My **V**ery **E**ducated **M**other **J**ust **S**erved **U**s **N**achos.

JUPITER

Jupiter is the largest planet in our solar system. It is mostly made of the gas hydrogen and does not have a solid surface.

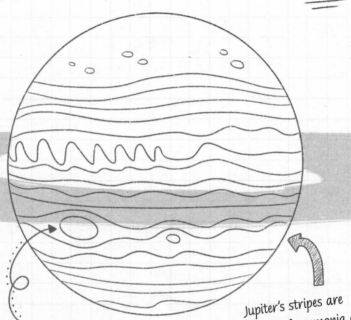

GIANT RED SPOT

Jupiter's Great Red Spot is a gigantic spinning storm. It's twice the size of Earth and has raged for hundreds of years.

Jupiter's stripes are clouds of ammonia and water. The clouds are very cold and windy.

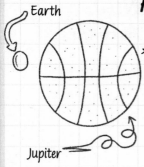
Earth

Jupiter

FACT FILE

* ***Size***: Jupiter is the largest planet in the solar system. You could fit 1,321 Earths inside Jupiter! If Earth were the size of a grape, Jupiter would be the size of a basketball.

* ***Distance from Sun***: Jupiter orbits about 484 million miles (778 million km) from the sun. Earth is 94 million miles (150 million km) away from the sun.

Jupiter's rings are made of dust.

* ***Moons***: Scientists now think Jupiter has 79 moons, but they're finding more all the time. The four biggest moons are Ganymede, Io, Callisto, and Europa.

A YEAR ON JUPITER IS THE SAME LENGTH AS 12 EARTH YEARS!

* ***Length of a day***: A day on Jupiter only lasts 10 hours—this is how long it takes to rotate on its axis.

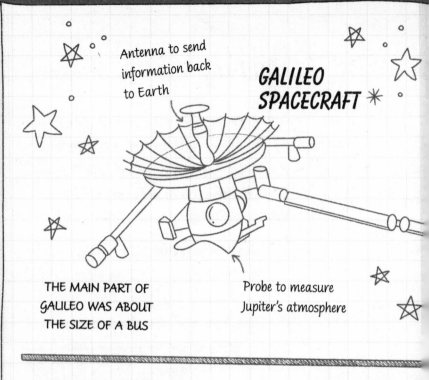

Antenna to send information back to Earth

GALILEO SPACECRAFT

THE MAIN PART OF GALILEO WAS ABOUT THE SIZE OF A BUS

Probe to measure Jupiter's atmosphere

MISSION TIMELINE

October 18, 1989
Galileo launches from Kennedy Space Center

February 10, 1990
Slingshots past Venus, using the planet's gravity to boost its speed

December 8, 1990
Flies by Earth, using its gravity to build speed

August 28, 1993
Visits an asteroid called Ida, discovering that it has its own tiny moon

July 22, 1994
Observes comet fragments impact Jupiter

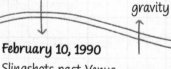

THE GALILEO MISSION

Four spacecraft had previously flown by Jupiter, but Galileo was the first to orbit the planet. Galileo studied Jupiter and its moons and sent information back to Earth. When a comet collided with Jupiter, Galileo recorded valuable information about the event.

Antenna to gather information

September 7, 1996
Discovers that Europa, one of Jupiter's biggest moons, has an ocean of water

September 21, 2003
Plunges into the blazing hot atmosphere of Jupiter and is destroyed

December 7, 1995
Enters orbit around Jupiter. A probe descends into the atmosphere and sends back data for an hour before it is destroyed.

October 15, 2001
Makes closest flyby of Io, passing just 112 miles (180km) above the surface

121

QUIZ

1   What's the name of the giant storm on Jupiter?

2   How many times could Earth fit into Jupiter?

3   Does Jupiter have rings?

4   How many moons does Jupiter have?

5   What is Jupiter's largest moon called?

6   Which of Jupiter's moons has got saltwater oceans?

7   Who was the first human being to
        walk on the moon?

8   What is the temperature at the
        center of the Earth?

SEARCH FOR JUPITER!

There are nine hidden Jupiter
stickers to spot in this book.
Can you find them all?

The stickers look
like this!

Check your answers on page 127

GLOSSARY

AIRLOCK

a special chamber that stops air from escaping from inside a spaceship into space

ANTENNA

a device used to transmit and receive radio signals

ASTEROIDS

small rocky objects that orbit the sun

COCKPIT

area near the front of a spacecraft where the pilot controls the craft

COMETS

lumps of ice and dust in space

GRAVITY

a force that pulls objects together. The Earth's gravity keeps us on the ground!

METEORITE

a piece of
space debris
that has smashed
into a planet's
surface

MICROBES

tiny living
creatures that
can only be
seen with a
microscope

MICROSCOPE

a scientific
instrument used
to see tiny objects

MILKY WAY

the galaxy that
contains our
solar system

ORBIT

the path of an
object around a
star, planet, or moon

PROBE

an unmanned
robotic spacecraft
that explores space

TELESCOPE

a tool that allows
people to see
faraway objects

THE GREAT RED SPOT

a giant storm in Jupiter's atmosphere

RETRO-ROCKETS

rockets attached to a spacecraft that help slow it down

SHOCK WAVES

a special, very strong, type of vibration coming from one spot

SLINGSHOT

when a spacecraft uses the gravity of a planet to increase its speed

SOLAR SYSTEM

the system of planets and other objects orbiting the sun

SPACE DUST

dust in space from comets, asteroids, and stars. Jupiter's rings are made of dust

SPACE SUIT
a suit worn by astronauts that allows them to survive in space

SPACE WALK
when astronauts go outside their spacecraft

VELOCITY
the speed of an object in one direction

Quiz answers

1. The Great Red Spot
2. 1,321
3. Yes
4. 79
5. Ganymede
6. Europa
7. Neil Armstrong
8. 10,800°F

For Conall, space expert and voyager among the stars

Text for DK by Working Partners Ltd
9 Kingsway, London WC2B 6XF
With special thanks to Adrian Bott

Design by Collaborate Ltd
Illustrator Ellie O'Shea
Consultant Sophie Allan

Acquisitions Editor Sam Priddy
Senior Commissioning Designer Joanne Clark
US Editor Margaret Parrish
US Senior Editor Shannon Beatty
Senior Production Editor Nikoleta Parasaki
Senior Producer Ena Matagic
Publishing Director Sarah Larter

First American Edition, 2020
Published in the United States by DK Publishing
1450 Broadway, Suite 801 New York, New York 10018

ISBN 978-0-7440-2106-6 (Paperback)
ISBN 978-0-7440-2385-5 (Hardcover)

DK books are available at special discounts when purchased in bulk for sales
promotions, premiums, fund-raising, or educational use. For details, contact: DK
Publishing Special Markets, 1450 Broadway, Suite 801, New York, New York 10018
SpecialSales@dk.com

Printed and bound in Great Britain by
Clays Ltd, Elcograf S.p.A.

All images © Dorling Kindersley Limited
For further information see: www.dkimages.com

For the curious
www.dk.com

The publisher would like to thank: Sally Beets and Seeta Parmar for editorial assistance;
and Caroline Twomey for proofreading.